First published in the English language 2009 by order of the Tate Trustees
by Tate Publishing, a division of Tate Enterprises Ltd,
Millbank, London SW1P 4RG
www.tate.org.uk/publishing

First published as *Des Jours pas comme les autres*
by Editions La Joie de lire SA, Geneva, 2006

© Editions La Joie de lire SA 2006
English language edition © Tate 2009

A catalogue record for this book is available from the British Library
ISBN 978-1-85437-850-7

Distributed in the United States and Canada by Harry N. Abrams, Inc., New York

Library of Congress Control Number: 2008931282

Printed in China

Taro Miura

CRAZY DAYS

Tate Publishing

The day the lighthouse went crazy

The day I was woken
by a tree full of music

SWING

The day I had fun with time

The day the train had a problem

The day the snow kept on falling

The day the band blew bubbles

The day the weathercock played in the breeze

The day I took off into the clouds

AIRPLANE

The day I was almost late

The day I went deep into the forest

 **The day I fell asleep under new sheets**

The day I found myself in the bathroom in the middle of the night